for Charlie

First American edition published in 1991 by
Peter Bedrick Books
2112 Broadway
New York, NY 10023
First published 1991 in Great Britain by Blackie and Son Ltd
Library of Congress Cataloging-in-Publication Data available
ISBN 0-87226-449-1

Printed in Hong Kong

Rub-a-Dub-Dub

77 Favorite Nursery Rhymes
compiled and illustrated by
Val Biro

Bedrick/Blackie
New York

CONTENTS

7

This little pig went to market,

This little pig stayed at home,

This little pig had roast beef,

This little pig had none.

And this little pig cried Wee-wee-wee
All the way home.

Rub-a-Dub-Dub,
Three men in a tub,
And how do you think they got there?
The butcher, the baker,
The candlestick-maker,
They all jumped out of a rotten potato,
'Twas enough to make a man stare.

To market, to market,
  To buy a fat pig,
Home again, home again,
  Jiggety-jig.

To market, to market,
  To buy a fat hog,
Home again, home again,
  Jiggety-jog.

A robin and a robin's son
  Once went to town to buy a bun.
They couldn't decide on plum or plain,
  And so they went back home again.

A farmer went trotting
  Upon his grey mare,
Bumpety, bumpety, bump!
With his daughter behind him,
  So rosy and fair,
Lumpety, lumpety, lump!

A raven cried, Croak!
  And they all tumbled down,
Bumpety, bumpety, bump!
The mare broke her knees,
  And the farmer his crown,
Lumpety, lumpety, lump!

The mischievous raven
  Flew laughing away,
Bumpety, bumpety, bump!
And vowed he would serve them
  The same the next day,
Lumpety, lumpety, lump!

This is the way the ladies ride,
  Nim, nim, nim, nim.
This is the way the gentlemen ride,
  Trim, trim, trim, trim.
This is the way the farmers ride,
  Trot, trot, trot, trot.
This is the way the huntsmen ride,
  A-gallop, a-gallop, a-gallop, a-gallop.
This is the way the ploughboys ride,
  Hobble-dy-gee, hobble-dy-gee.

A trot, and a canter, a gallop and over,
Out of the saddle, and roll in the clover.

Ride away, ride away,
  Johnny shall ride,
He shall have a pussy cat
  Tied to one side;
He shall have a little dog
  Tied to the other,
And Johnny shall ride
  To see his grandmother.

Ride a cock-horse to Banbury Cross
  To see a fine lady upon a white horse;
Rings on her fingers and bells on her toes,
  And she shall have music wherever she goes.

Solomon Grundy,
    Born on a Monday,
Christened on Tuesday,
    Married on Wednesday,
Took ill on Thursday,
    Worse on Friday,
Died on Saturday,
    Buried on Sunday:
This is the end
    Of Solomon Grundy.

As Tommy Snooks and Bessy
    Brooks
Were walking out one Sunday,
Says Tommy Snooks to Bessy
    Brooks,
Tomorrow will be Monday.

Humpty Dumpty sat on a wall,
Humpty Dumpty had a great fall;
All the King's horses and all the
King's men
Couldn't put Humpty together
again.

The Lion and the Unicorn
Were fighting for the crown;
The Lion beat the Unicorn
All around the town.

Some gave them white bread,
And some gave them brown;
Some gave them plum cake
And drummed them out
of town.

Up and down the City Road,
  In and out the Eagle,
That's the way the money goes,
  Pop goes the weasel!

Half a pound of tuppenny rice,
  Half a pound of treacle,
Mix it up and make it nice,
  Pop goes the weasel!

Yankee Doodle came to town,
  Riding on a pony;
He stuck a feather in his cap
  And called it macaroni.

Hey diddle, diddle,
  The cat and the fiddle,
The cow jumped over the moon;
  The little dog laughed
To see such sport,
  And the dish ran away with
    the spoon.

Pat-a-cake, pat-a-cake, baker's man,
  Make me a cake as fast as you can:
Pat it and prick it, and mark it with B,
  Toss it in the oven for Baby and me.

Cobbler, cobbler, mend my shoe,
Get it done by half-past two;
Stitch it up, and stitch it down,
Then I'll give you half-a-crown.

Bow-wow, says the dog,

Mew, mew, says the cat,

Grunt, grunt, goes the hog,

And squeak goes the rat.

Tu-whu, says the owl,

Caw, caw, says the crow,

Quack, quack, says the duck,

And what cuckoos say –
    you know!

Round and round the cornfield
    Looking for a hare;
Where can we find one?
    Right up there!

The Queen of Hearts,
    She made some tarts,
All on a summer's day;
    The Knave of Hearts
He stole those tarts,
    And took them clean away.

The King of Hearts
    Called for the tarts,
And beat the Knave full sore;
    The Knave of Hearts
Brought back the tarts,
    And vowed he'd steal no more.

21

There was a crooked man,
    And he walked a crooked mile,
He found a crooked sixpence,
    Upon a crooked stile;
He bought a crooked cat,
    Which caught a crooked mouse,
And they all lived together
    In a little crooked house.

Hoddley, poddley, puddle and fogs,
  Cats are to marry the poodle dogs;
Cats in blue jackets and dogs in
      red hats,
  What will become of the mice and
      the rats?

Higglety, pigglety, pop!
  The dog has eaten the mop;
The pig's in a hurry,
  The cat's in a flurry,
Higglety, pigglety, pop!

Pussy cat, pussy cat,
 Where have you been?
I've been to London
 To look at the Queen.
Pussy cat, pussy cat,
 What did you there?
I frightened a little mouse
 Under her chair.

Mary had a little lamb
   Its fleece was white as snow;
And everywhere that Mary went
   The lamb was sure to go.

It followed her to school one day
   Which was against the rule;
It made the children laugh and play
   To see a lamb at school.

And so the teacher turned it out
   But still it lingered near,
And waited patiently about
   Till Mary did appear.

What makes the lamb love Mary so?
   The eager children cry;
Why, Mary loves the lamb, you know
   The teacher did reply.

Old Mother Hubbard
     Went to the cupboard,
To fetch her poor dog a bone;
     But when she got there,
     The cupboard was bare
And so the poor dog had none.

She went to the baker's
     To buy him some bread;
But when she came back
     The poor dog was dead.

She went to the fishmonger's
     To buy him some fish;
But when she came back
     He was licking the dish.

She went to the joiner's
     To buy him a coffin;
But when she came back
     The poor dog was laughing.

She went to the tavern
     For white wine and red;
But when she came back
     The dog stood on his head.

She took a clean dish
     To get him some tripe;
But when she came back
     He was smoking a pipe.

She went to the fruiterer's
     To buy him some fruit;
But when she came back
     He was playing the flute.

She went to the tailor's
    To buy him a coat;
But when she came back
    He was riding a goat.

She went to the hatter's
    To buy him a hat;
But when she came back
    He was feeding the cat.

She went to the barber's
    To buy him a wig;
But when she came back
    He was dancing a jig.

She went to the cobbler's
    To buy him some shoes;
But when she came back
    He was reading the news.

She went to the seamstress
    To buy him some linen;
But when she came back
    The dog was a-spinning.

She went to the hosier's
    To buy him some hose;
But when she came back
    He was dressed in his clothes.

The dame made a curtsey,
    The dog made a bow;
The dame said, Your servant,
    The dog said, Bow-wow.

Georgie Porgie, pudding and pie,
  Kissed the girls and made them cry;
When the boys came out to play,
  Georgie Porgie ran away.

There was a man of Thessaly
  And he was wondrous wise,
He jumped into a bramble bush
  And scratched out both his eyes.
And when he saw his eyes were out,
  With all his might and main
He jumped into another bush
  And scratched them in again.

Hickory, dickory, dock,
   The mouse ran up the clock.
The clock struck one,
   The mouse ran down,
Hickory, dickory, dock.

Six little mice sat down to spin;
   Pussy passed by and she peeped in.
What are you doing, my little men?
   Weaving coats for gentlemen.
Shall I come in and cut off your threads?
   No, no, Mistress Pussy, you'd bite off
            our heads.
Oh no, I'll not; I'll help you spin.
   That may be so, but you don't come in.

Mary, Mary, quite contrary,
How does your garden grow?
With silver bells and cockle-shells,
And pretty maids all in a row.

Charley, Charley,
Stole the barley
Out of the baker's shop.
The baker came out
And gave him a clout,
Which made poor Charley hop.

Tweedledum and Tweedledee
  Agreed to have a battle,
For Tweedledum said Tweedledee
  Had spoiled his nice new rattle.
Just then flew down a monstrous crow
  As black as a tar-barrel,
Which frightened both the heroes so,
  They quite forgot their quarrel.

Jack and Jill went up the hill
To fetch a pail of water;
Jack fell down
and broke his crown,
And Jill came tumbling after.

Diddle, diddle, dumpling, my son John,
Went to bed with his trousers on;
One shoe off and one shoe on,
Diddle, diddle, dumpling, my son John.

Diddlety, diddlety, dumpty,
    The cat ran up the plum-tree;
Half a crown to fetch her down,
Diddlety, diddlety, dumpty.

Then up Jack got
        and home did trot
    As fast as he could caper;
And went to bed
        to mend his head
    With vinegar and brown paper.

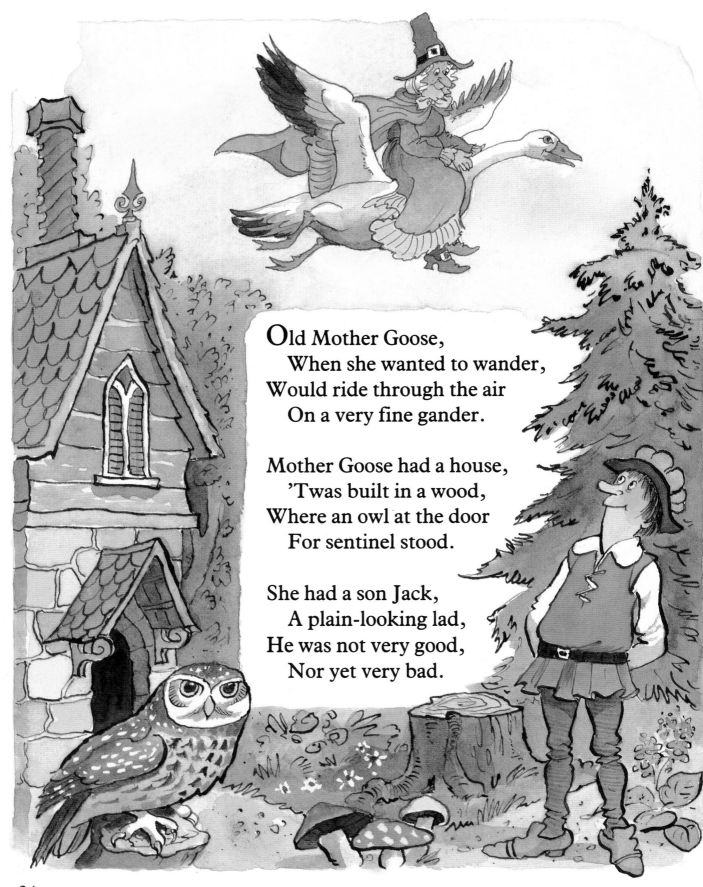

Old Mother Goose,
    When she wanted to wander,
Would ride through the air
    On a very fine gander.

Mother Goose had a house,
    'Twas built in a wood,
Where an owl at the door
    For sentinel stood.

She had a son Jack,
    A plain-looking lad,
He was not very good,
    Nor yet very bad.

She sent him to market,
    A live goose he bought;
See, mother, says he,
    I have not been for nought.

Jack's goose and her gander
    Grew very fond;
They'd both eat together,
    Or swim in the pond.

Jack found one fine morning
    As I have been told,
His goose had laid him
    An egg of pure gold.

I saw a ship a-sailing,
  A-sailing on the sea,
And oh, but it was laden
  With pretty things for thee!

There were comfits in the cabin,
  And apples in the hold;
The sails were made of silk,
  And the masts were all of gold.

The four-and-twenty sailors
  That stood between the decks,
Were four-and-twenty white mice
  With chains about their necks.

The captain was a duck
  With a packet on his back,
And when the ship began to move
  The captain said, Quack! Quack!

I had a little pony,
  His name was Dapple Gray;
I lent him to a lady
  To ride a mile away.
She whipped him, she slashed him,
  She rode him through the mire;
I would not lend my pony now
  For all the lady's hire.

Twinkle, twinkle, little star,
How I wonder what you are!
Up above the world so high,
Like a diamond in the sky.

Christmas is coming,
The geese are getting fat,
Please to put a penny
In the old man's hat.
If you haven't got a penny,
A ha'penny will do;
If you haven't got a ha'penny,
Then God bless you!

Jack Sprat could eat no fat,
His wife could eat no lean;
And so betwixt them both, you see,
They licked the platter clean.

Jack ate all the lean,
Joan ate all the fat,
The bone they picked it clean
And gave it to the cat.

ORANGES AND LEMONS

Gay go up and gay go down,
To ring the bells of London Town.

Bull's eyes and targets,
Say the bells of St Marg'ret's.

Brickbats and tiles,
Say the bells of St Giles'.

Oranges and lemons,
Say the bells of St Clement's.

Pancakes and fritters,
Say the bells of St Peter's.

Two sticks and an apple,
Say the bells of Whitechapel.

Old Father Baldpate,
Say the slow bells at Aldgate.

Maids in white aprons,
Say the bells of St Catherine's.

Pokers and tongs,
Say the bells of St John's.

Kettles and pans,
Say the bells of St Anne's.

You owe me five farthings,
Say the bells of St Martin's.

When will you pay me?
Say the bells at Old Bailey.

When I grow rich,
Say the bells at Shoreditch.

Pray, when will that be?
Say the bells at Stepney.

I'm sure I don't know,
Says the great bell at Bow.

HERE COMES A CANDLE TO LIGHT YOU TO BED,
HERE COMES A CHOPPER TO CHOP OFF YOUR HEAD.

Dickery, dickery, dare,
　The pig flew up in the air;
The man in brown
Soon brought him down,
　Dickery, dickery, dare.

Hickety, pickety, my black hen,
　She lays eggs for gentlemen;
Gentlemen come every day
　To see what my black hen doth lay.

There was an old woman who lived in a shoe,
   She had so many children she didn't know what to do;
She gave them some broth without any bread;
   She whipped them all soundly and sent them to bed.

Little Miss Muffet
    Sat on a tuffet,
Eating her curds and whey;
    There came a big spider,
Who sat down beside her
    And frightened Miss
        Muffet away.

Polly put the kettle on,
    Polly put the kettle on,
Polly put the kettle on,
    We'll all have tea.

Sukey take it off again,
    Sukey take it off again,
Sukey take it off again,
    They've all gone away.

Sing a song of sixpence,
    A pocket full of rye;
Four-and-twenty blackbirds,
    Baked in a pie.

When the pie was opened,
    The birds began to sing;
Was not that a dainty dish
    To set before a king?

The king was in his counting-house
   Counting out his money;
The Queen was in the parlour,
   Eating bread and honey.

The maid was in the garden
   Hanging out the clothes,
When down came a blackbird
   And pecked off her nose.

Goosey, goosey, gander,
  Whither shall I wander?
Upstairs and downstairs
  And in my lady's chamber.

There I met an old man
  Who would not say his prayers,
I took him by the left leg
  And threw him down the stairs.

Baa, baa, black sheep,
  Have you any wool?
Yes sir, yes sir,
  Three bags full;
One for the master,
  One for the dame,
And one for the little boy
  Who lives down the lane.

46

O, the grand old Duke of York,
He had ten thousand men;
He marched them up to the top of the hill
And he marched them down again!

And when they were up they were up,
And when they were down they were down,
And when they were only half-way up,
They were neither up nor down.

Old King Cole
Was a merry old soul,
And a merry old soul was he;
He called for his pipe,
And he called for his bowl,
And he called for his
fiddlers three.

Now every fiddler
He had a fiddle,
And a very fine fiddle had he;
Oh, there's none so rare
As can compare
With King Cole and his
fiddlers three!

Tom, Tom, the piper's son,
Stole a pig and away he run;
The pig was eat,
And Tom was beat,
And Tom went howling
Down the street.

Little Jack Horner
Sat in a corner,
Eating a Christmas pie;
He put in his thumb
And pulled out a plum,
And said, What a
good boy am I!

A wise old owl sat in an oak,
The more he heard the less he spoke;
The less he spoke the more he heard.
Why aren't we all like that wise old bird?

There was a jolly miller once,
Lived on the river Dee;
He worked and sang from morn till
night,
No lark more blithe than he.
And this the burden of his song
Forever used to be,
I care for nobody, no! not I,
And nobody cares for me.

Where are you going to, my pretty maid?
  I'm going a-milking, sir, she said.

May I go with you, my pretty maid?
  You're kindly welcome, sir, she said.

Say, will you marry me, my pretty maid?
  Yes, if you please, kind sir, she said.

What is your father, my pretty maid?
  My father's a farmer, sir, she said.

What is your fortune, my pretty maid?
  My face is my fortune, sir, she said.

Then I can't marry you, my pretty maid.
  Nobody asked you, sir, she said.

There was an old woman tossed up in a basket,
  Seventeen times as high as the moon;
Where she was going I couldn't but ask it,
  For in her hand she carried a broom.

Old woman, old woman, old woman, quoth I,
  Where are you going to up so high?
To brush the cobwebs off the sky!
  May I go with you? Aye, by-and-by.

Three blind mice, see how they run!
They all ran after the farmer's wife,
Who cut off their tails with a carving knife,
Did you ever hear such a thing in your life,
　　As three blind mice?

Little Bo-peep has lost her sheep,
　　And doesn't know where to find them;
Leave them alone, and they'll come home,
　　Bringing their tails behind them.

53

It's raining, it's pouring,
  The old man's snoring,
He got into bed
  And bumped his head,
And couldn't get up in the
  morning.

Rain on the green grass,
  And rain on the tree,
Rain on the house-top,
  But not on me.

Doctor Foster went to Gloucester
    In a shower of rain;
He stepped in a puddle,
    Right up to his middle,
And never went there again.

I do not like thee, Doctor Fell,
    The reason why I cannot tell;
But this I know, and know full well,
    I do not like thee, Doctor Fell.

Two legs sat upon three legs
  With one leg in his lap;

In comes four legs,
  Runs away with one leg,

Up jumps two legs,
  Picks up three legs,

Throws it after four legs,
  And makes him bring
            back one leg.

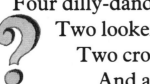

Four stiff-standers,
  Four dilly-danders,
    Two lookers,
      Two crookers,
        And a wig-wag.

Tinker,
   Tailor,
Soldier,
   Sailor,
Rich man,
   Poor man,
Beggar man,
Thief.

One, two, three, four, five,
   Once I caught a fish alive.
Six, seven, eight, nine, ten,
   Then I let it go again.
Why did you let it go?
   Because it bit my finger so.
Which finger did it bite?
   This little finger on the right.

The man in the wilderness asked me
   How many strawberries grew in the sea.
I answered him as I thought good,
   As many as red herrings grew in the wood.

TONGUE TWISTERS

Peter Piper picked a peck of
     pickled pepper;
A peck of pickled pepper Peter
     Piper picked.
If Peter Piper picked a peck of
     pickled pepper,
Where's the peck of pickled pepper
     Peter Piper picked?

Moses supposes his toeses are roses,
   But Moses supposes erroneously;
For nobody's toeses are posies of roses
   As Moses supposes his toeses to be.

The man in the moon
Came down too soon,
And asked his way to Norwich;

He went by the South
And burnt his mouth
With supping cold plum porridge.

Wee Willie Winkie
    runs through the town,
Upstairs and downstairs
    in his nightgown,
Rapping at the window,
    crying through the lock,
Are the children all in bed?
    It's past eight o'clock.

The cock doth crow
To let you know
If you be wise
'Tis time to rise:
For early to bed,
And early to rise,
Is the way to be healthy
And wealthy and wise.

Three wise men of Gotham
Went to sea in a bowl;
And if the bowl had been stronger,
My tale would have been longer.

I'll tell you a story
About Jack a Nory,
And now my story's
begun;

I'll tell you another
Of Jack and his brother;
And now my story
is done.

The End